TH

By the same author in Piccolo

THE GREAT FIRE
FOLLYFOOT
DORA AT FOLLYFOOT
THE HOUSE AT WORLD'S END
SUMMER AT WORLD'S END
WORLD'S END IN WINTER

THE GREAT ESCAPE

MONICA DICKENS

Cover and text illustrations by Michael Jackson

A Piccolo Book

PAN BOOKS LTD
LONDON AND SYDNEY

First published 1971 by Kaye and Ward Ltd
This edition published 1974 by Pan Books Ltd,
Cavaye Place, London SW10 9PG

ISBN 0 330 24065 X

Made and printed in Great Britain by
Cox & Wyman Ltd, London, Reading and Fakenham

Chapter One

When she woke up that morning in the tall grey Paris house on the bank of the River Seine, Chantal knew at once that something terrible was happening.

Something terrible even for these violent times. For the last three years, Paris had been torn and shocked by the French Revolution. The peasants and workers had risen up in anger and revenge against the rich aristocrats who wanted everything in France for themselves. They had rebelled against the fat King Louis the Sixteenth, and his spoiled Queen, Marie-Antoinette, who cared nothing for the ordinary working people.

Chantal was eleven years old, but it seemed as if the fighting and killing had been going on for as long as she could remember. Gone were all those sunny days when she had played as a little girl in the gardens and meadows of her rich father's country house. Gone were the

Chantal knew something terrible was happening

crisp Paris nights when she had driven to parties behind the two black horses with her elegant mother, both of them wrapped in soft furs.

Gone long ago, vanished like a dream. Now there were no party dresses, no games, no horses. Not even any sunshine any more. In that year of 1792, it always seemed to be raining, as if Paris was weeping for its prisoners and its dead.

It was raining this morning. The bedroom was full of a sad grey light, and the high windows were streaming. Chantal sat up quickly in bed. Shouting in the street outside. Women screaming. The clatter of many running feet on the cobblestones. Chantal ran across the cold, polished floor and peered between the lace curtains at the tall windows, although she had been taught not to look out at the street. Not when there was trouble. Not when the mob was angry and hunting for victims.

Chantal's father was an aristocrat, the Count of Previn, a top dog once, like the other French noblemen. Now they were looked on as the enemies of the revolutionary people, who hated them as much as they hated the King and Queen.

The bedroom door opened and her mother, the Countess, came in. When she saw Chantal looking out, she came quickly across the room and pulled her back.

'Stay away from the windows! Haven't you been told?' Usually, she was a kind mother with a gentle voice like evening birds, but fear made her talk sharply.

'Why? What's outside there? Why is there so much noise? What's happening, Mama?'

'What's happening? Everything. Cruelty and horror. Disaster and tragedy.' The Countess spread out her hands, making words in the air in the way French people do, as if they are conducting the orchestra of life. 'The people are like mad dogs. They stormed through the streets, singing that new song, the *Marseillaise*: "The day of glory has come" – Glory! This is a day of disgrace. They have attacked the Palace of the Tuileries. They murdered all the Royal guards and locked up the King and Queen and their children.'

'Will they be killed?' Three years of living with the Revolution had taught Chantal to think of this at once. So many people had been killed. Some of their relations and friends. Even helpless old people and children. Children she had played with in that other beautiful life of games and laughter and music which she could hardly remember.

'Hush. I don't know.' Her mother was jumpy and nervous. 'Get dressed now.'

'But will they?' Chantal had her father's stubborn nature. When she wanted something, she went after it with her hands clenched and her chin stuck out.

'Hush, darling.'

'I'm not a baby. *Tell me.*'

Her mother helped her to dress in her blue dress with the white collar and starched apron, but she would not answer any more questions.

Chapter Two

As soon as she could get away from the lessons which her mother set for her every day since her governess had run away to join the Revolution, Chantal slipped out to the big kitchen to talk to the servants. They were her best companions, now that nearly all her friends and cousins had run away or disappeared.

The cook was crying into the soup. 'Not because I'm sorry for that devil and witch, Queen Marie-Antoinette, but because I'm making onion soup.'

'What will happen to the King and Queen?' Chantal turned to Marcel, the manservant. She did not like him, but he knew all the answers.

'What do *you* think?' With a hideous gesture, and a noise like tearing cotton cloth, Marcel ran his finger across his throat like the sharp knife of the guillotine, the dreadful machine which chopped off heads in the big open Square across the river. 'Madame Guillotine isn't fussy. King or carpenter, she eats 'em all.'

That was the sort of thing he thought funny. His laugh was like dirty bathwater gurgling down into the underworld.

He was a dark, slinky man who walked like a cat. He could come up behind you in the shadows of a passage and pinch you, then give that bloodcurdling laugh to cover your yelp, so that your parents would think it was only a joke.

'How do *you* know who goes to the guillotine?' Chantal asked as rudely as she dared, and keeping safely on the other side of the big scrubbed wood table where he was polishing silver. 'Are you the leader of the Revolution?'

'No, Mademoiselle.' Marcel took a drink from the glass at his elbow. Chantal knew he stole her father's wine, but she had never told. He bowed over the valuable salt cellar, carved like a Viking's boat, which he was polishing. 'No, I am only the faithful servant of the Count and Countess, your noble parents.'

His face was smooth and secret, like a cat that cannot smile.

Looking down the stone passage to the back of the house, Chantal could see that her friend Lisette, the washerwoman, had come with her big basket for the laundry. Her son Philippe would be out in the courtyard with

Chantal slipped out to the big kitchen

the horse and cart. Chantal gave him a whistle. She could only whistle down here in the kitchen part of the house. Upstairs it was all right to sing, but nice young ladies did not whistle.

She went down the passage. Lisette was a small, chirpy woman with a braid of brown hair round her head like a wreath. Her red cheeks were always spread in a cheerful smile, but today her bright face was set with worry.

'What's happening?' Chantal asked. Lisette lived among the crowds in the middle of the city and knew all the news and gossip. 'Are they going to kill the King and Queen?'

'Who knows? They have killed all his soldiers at the Palace.'

'And all his horses too,' Philippe called from the yard where he was mending the bridle of the old bay horse with a piece of string.

'Why? Didn't they want to use them?'

'They wanted even more to eat them.' Philippe was a little older than Chantal and had lived all his life in the dirty crowded alleys and slums among the poor of Paris. Nothing surprised him.

'Oh!' Chantal's eyes were as round as coat buttons. She put her fingers in her mouth because she had to bite her nails when she was upset. 'Are the people really so hungry?'

'Listen, Mademoiselle Chantal, listen. You're a rich man's child. You've always had food and clothes and a warm fire. A big soft bed. A doctor when you were ill. You don't know. You can't imagine . . .'

Bending over the pile of laundry, sorting sheets and shirts and fine embroidered petticoats, Lisette began to talk quietly and bitterly, talking of the truth.

Chapter Three

When Marcel sounded the brass gong to call Chantal to the dining table with her parents, she began to talk at once.

'Lisette has been telling me how terrible it's been for the poor peasants all these years. How badly the aristocrats treated the working people, making them pay all the taxes, not letting them earn enough money or have enough to eat. Did you know, Papa, that in the city, they had to work a whole day to buy two loaves of bread? In the country, Lisette said, the corn her sister planted was eaten by the rich baron's tame pigeons. Her children were so hungry they would scratch in the earth like animals, digging for roots. And the rich baron rode by on his jingling horse and laughed at them.'

'I know.' Her father nodded sadly. 'It's true.'

'But you were never like that, Papa!' She stretched out her hand to him and knocked over the pepper-pot without noticing. 'You were always good to the people who worked for you.' Her father had once owned a big house in the country, and farms and cattle and horses, all now seized by the Revolutionaries. 'All the farm-hands and the servants, in the country and in town, they all loved you.'

He spread his hands. 'Who knows?'

'They *did*.' Chantal turned to the man-servant. 'Didn't they, Marcel?'

'Of course.' Marcel picked up the pepper-pot. He was serving the food, silently and smoothly, with his usual secret face that did not show whether he hoped they would enjoy it or not.

'No one must suspect anything,' Marcel said

'But we're aristocrats. That's enough.' The Count shrugged his shoulders. 'To the people of the Revolution, we're now the enemy.'

'I'm afraid.' The Countess was not eating anything. Chantal looked across the table and saw that she was crying. 'After today . . . the King and Queen. I'm afraid we're in new danger.'

'Would they arrest us too, Mama?'

'Of course not. Eat your onion soup.' Chantal's father was trying to seem calm, but she saw his nervous mouth under the dark moustache and how his fingers drummed on the table, and she thought that if he were a woman instead of a man, he might be crying too.

'If I may speak?' Marcel padded across the carpet to shut the door which led to the kitchen and came close to the table. 'The Countess is right. There is danger for you, as there is for all the aristocrats who were friends of the King. But if you'll let me, I believe I can help you.'

'How? There are barricades in the streets. All the gates in the city walls are guarded. There's no escaping Paris. Our only chance is to stay here and wait, and be brave, and hope that one day things will get better.'

'They won't.' Marcel shook his sleek, black head. 'They'll get worse. But I think I know someone who can help you. Listen, I know a man . . .'

And so, after a lot of secret talk, the escape was all planned for the next day.

They must beware of spies. They were probably being watched now. They had been fairly safe as long as they stayed at home in Paris, but if they were caught planning to escape, they would all be seized at once.

And so they must pretend that tomorrow was just an ordinary day. They must get up at the same time, dress the same, have breakfast. The house must be just the same, with the Count in his study, writing his memoirs of his father, who had been a famous general. The Countess would be sewing, Chantal doing her lessons, the cook cooking and the maid sweeping, the washerwoman Lisette coming to fetch the white lace window curtains, since it was the regular curtain-washing day.

'No one must suspect anything,' Marcel said. 'There are spies everywhere.' He glanced over his shoulder into the chimney corner, as if he expected someone to be crouching in the tall, tiled stove. 'In these terrible times when the people are like mad dogs, hungry for blood, even your friends will betray you. But not me. Not Marcel. You've been good to me. You've treated me well. I will repay you with your lives.'

'Thank you, Marcel.' Chantal's mother laid her small, white hand on his arm. 'You're a true friend.'

'But you run a risk yourself,' Papa said anxiously.

'I know.' Marcel tried to put on a brave and noble expression, but it would not fit on his sharp face. 'But I'll do my best to help you. I give you my word.'

They shook hands. 'Thank you,' Papa said. 'We'll never forget it.'

Chantal stuffed a big piece of bread into her mouth so that she would not have to say anything. She wished Marcel were not so creepy and hateful, with his cold cat's eyes and thin, unsmiling mouth. She wished that it could be anyone but Marcel who was going to save their lives.

Chapter Four

The next day Chantal's father dressed in his blue silk waistcoat and knee breeches and his ruffled shirt and white cravat, as if he were going to spend the day in his study, not in the adventure of escape.

Her mother told the maid to take down the curtains for the washerwoman. Then she spent a long time prettily piling up her red-gold hair, and put on her pearl necklace and her pale lilac dress with the stiff hoop under the skirt, as if she might be going out to visit a friend, not running away to a secret and dangerous hiding place.

Chantal put on her blue dress and white apron and sat down to study. As if books mattered any more. As if it was important to put anything into your head when the only thing that really mattered was not getting it cut off by the guillotine.

Marcel was very nervous. He kept going to

the windows, stepping out into the courtyard at the back of the house, peering down the side street. When Lisette and Philippe clopped into the yard with their old bay horse and ricketty wagon, he did not stroke his nasty little moustache as he usually did and stand on his toes to seem taller, and try to flirt with the bright-cheeked washerwoman. He ducked back into the house, as if he thought Lisette herself might be a spy.

'Isn't it time?' the Count and Countess kept asking him. 'Isn't it time to go?'

'Not yet.' Marcel put his finger to his lips. 'Wait. Trust me.'

So they waited. And they trusted. And just before noon, with a terrifying crash of splintering wood and glass, the soldiers of the Revolution broke down the front door with the ends of their heavy muskets, clattered up the stairs and seized the Count and Countess before they had time to run or hide.

'Chantal!' Mama's voice was the most terrible, heart-tearing shriek her daughter had ever heard. 'My child – oh, save the child!'

As she was dragged away by the rough men, her fine dress torn, her hair tumbling round

The soldiers seized the Count and Countess

her desperate face, her eyes implored Marcel.

'Listen to that,' he said calmly. 'So the rats in the trap squeal.' His laugh was like a murderous demon. His smile was a slice of wickedness. The only time Chantal had ever seen him smile.

The Count had understood. 'You – Marcel – you traitor!' he shouted, before a soldier put a filthy hand over his mouth and dragged him struggling down the stairs.

'And the little mouse will squeal too.' Marcel quickly bent and lifted the flounce of the high sofa where Chantal had often hidden for fun when she was little. 'Got you!' He grabbed. She bit his disgusting hand. He yelled. She wriggled out between his legs and he fell backwards into a glass cabinet full of ornaments.

Before he could struggle up from the broken glass and china, Chantal was out of the room. She ran down the back stairs, through the kitchen where the cook had her apron over her head and the maid was hiding in the flour barrel with the lid on her head and only her scared eyes showing, and out into the courtyard.

Chantal ran down the back stairs

'Quick – into the basket!' Without thought or question, Lisette pushed her roughly into the big laundry basket and piled on the heavy lace curtains, just in time, as Marcel ran out of the back door, panting and cursing.

'Where's that child?' he shouted. 'I want the aristocrats' child.'

'The soldiers got her,' Lisette answered. Chantal, trembling and afraid in the scratchy wicker basket, half smothered by the curtains, was amazed at how calm Lisette's voice was.

'Ah, good. That will be the end of her tricks, that young lady.' Again the awful sound in his throat to imitate the sharp hissing blade of the guillotine.

'Stop acting and showing off, Marcel,' Lisette said, 'and help me with this heavy basket.'

'Why should I?' His voice was coarse and drunken. He must have been at the Count's wine while he was waiting for the soldiers. 'Their curtains and everything else can be thrown in the mud now.'

'It's all right for you,' Lisette grumbled. 'You're well enough off, with all the wine and food and money you've stolen from the Count all this time. I'm a poor woman. I can sell these curtains. Isn't that the least that's due to me after breaking my back and ruining my hands at the washtub for these lazy, spoiled aristocrats?'

'Ah, yes.' That was the sort of talk Marcel understood.

Frightened as she was, Chantal could still smile to herself that it was Marcel himself, the wicked, cunning traitor, who lifted one end of the basket and dumped her into the back of the cart that carried her – clop-clop of the stiff old horse, creak-squeak of the rusty wheels – away from his clutches.

Chapter Five

Lisette and Philippe lived in what had once been a grand house on the other side of the river. In these violent days of the Revolution, when so many rich people and nobles were being arrested and often put to death, their houses were taken over by swarms of people from the slums of Paris, many of whom had never lived in a real house with a proper roof over their heads.

Fifteen or twenty families would move into one house, each family grabbing a room, breaking up the furniture for firewood, eating the food in the cellars, drinking the wine and smashing the priceless ornaments and paintings just for the fun of it.

In Lisette's house some of the rooms had a dozen people living in them, chattering, sleeping, cooking, quarrelling. She and Philippe were lucky to have a room to themselves at the back of the ground floor.

Chantal crept stiffly out of the laundry basket in the cold, stone-floored room which had once been a nobleman's kitchen, where banquets were prepared in the old days, and a crowd of underpaid servants worked to stuff with rich food the over-stuffed stomachs of the rich. Frightened, miserable, lost, bruised and sick from the jolting ride in the cart, she burst into tears and sobbed, 'I want my mother! I want to go home!'

Lisette took her in her arms and comforted her, stroking her tousled, copper-coloured hair. She did not say anything about her mother, but she said, 'This is your home. You can stay with us.'

'No! I want to go home!' Chantal knew she was behaving like a baby, but she was desperate. Her mind and eyes were full of the last sight of her dear mother and father, dragged away by the brutal soldiers. She went on sobbing.

'Be quiet.' Lisette tried to calm her. 'The neighbours . . . Oh, Philippe, what can I do with her? Hush, Chantal. Please.'

Philippe, who had always been polite to Chantal and rather shy of her, because she was the Count's daughter and he was the washerwoman's son, strode across the room and began to shake her. 'Shut up,' he said roughly. 'We saved your life.'

Chantal was shocked into silence. She went into a corner by the stove and sat brooding like a chicken, hunched up and ruffled. She was fighting with her pride, trying to make herself do something she did not want to do. After a while, she came and put her arms round Lisette, who was small and slender like Mama, but her skin was rougher and she did not smell so nice.

'I'm sorry,' Chantal whispered. 'Thank you.'

After that she did what she was told. She took off her neat blue dress with the starched white collar and apron and put on a ragged brown smock and a pair of wooden clogs on her soft clean feet.

'Better dirty those up a bit.' Philippe took some ashes from the stove and rubbed them over her toes. It tickled, and so luckily Chantal was giggling when one of the neighbours from upstairs looked in.

She was a busybody woman with a sharp

nose and eyes like black beetles that darted about everywhere, looking for trouble. 'Who's that child?' she asked. 'What's *she* doing here?

'She's my cousin,' Philippe answered quickly.

'Yes,' said Lisette, catching on at once. 'My sister's daughter from the country. Out in

'Who's that child?' the neighbour asked

Saint Cloud, you know, where I go every week to fetch eggs and vegetables.'

The three of them held their breath. The busybody neighbour peered, sniffed, drew down her nose and pushed out her bottom lip as if she was trying to make them meet, and finally said, 'She's very pale for a country child.'

'She's been ill,' Lisette invented.

'Then why bring her to this town of pestilence and pox? I suppose your sister is more interested in selling her eggs and chickens than in feeding her own daughter,' said the neighbour, and went off, imagining that she had scored a point.

Chapter Six

As the days went by, and then the weeks, Chantal learned to talk in the rougher way of the street children. Her hair was unbrushed and her face dirty. After eleven years of being prim and neat and clean and ladylike, she really enjoyed being able to climb and play and fight without caring about clothes and manners among the gangs of children who roamed Paris like young brigands.

Once a week Lisette dumped her in the big copper of hot water in the wash-house that stood in the back yard. She was still working as a washerwoman, doing laundry mostly for soldiers now that so many of her old customers were gone: here one day, like Chantal's mother and father, and vanished the next.

The Count and Countess of Previn had been taken to the prison on the island in the middle of the River Seine. It was called the Palace of Justice, but there was no justice there. People were condemned and locked up without a trial. The only way out was the way that led to the guillotine.

Every day Chantal went across the bridge in her grubby smock and her wooden clogs and walked outside the prison walls, whistling old favourite songs of her childhood, looking at all the barred windows, hoping to see a beloved face.

She sang:

All the birds are singing together,
They say it's the end of the cold winter weather . . .

And the clapping song from long ago:

Co-Co was a naughty boy,
Co-Co was a brat,
Co-Co took his mutton soup
And threw it at the cat.

'Perhaps they can hear me.' Back at home, she sat on an upturned bucket in a corner of the old stable which Philippe had made into a forge. His father had been a blacksmith and had taught him how to shoe a horse and make hinges and tools out of iron bars. 'Do you think they know it's me?'

'There's no one who can whistle like you.'

It was her best trick. She could whistle

better than a boy, and imitate all kinds of birds.

'But suppose they're not there?'

Philippe did not know what to say. He blew up the fire with the bellows until his face glowed as red as the iron shoe he was heating.

'Suppose they're dead?'

He shook his head and bent to pick up the foot of the water carrier's pony, holding the hot shoe against it with a stinging smell of burning hoof.

'You'd know if they were dead.' He spoke with his head against the pony's side because it was easier to talk about this without looking at Chantal. 'I knew when my father was killed. I was chopping wood for my mother. Suddenly I heard his voice calling me. "Philippe", he said, not shouting or excited. Just "Philippe" like that, as if he liked to say my name. I looked up, but of course he wasn't there. He was lying in the street in the rain.'

'Who killed him?'

'A drunken young aristocrat. A friend of ours saw what happened. He galloped round a corner, whipping up his horse. My father ran to get out of the way, slipped on the wet cobbles and fell, and the drunken fool drove over him without even looking back.'

'Oh!' Chantal had her hands over her face, as if the terrible thing were happening now. 'How could he?'

'That's the way it was in those days.' Philippe put down the pony's hoof and began to hammer at the shoe on the anvil. 'That's why there had to be a Revolution.'

'I can't believe it.'

'It's true. Rich aristocrats like that thought they owned the world. Not your parents, of course.' He plunged the hot shoe into a bucket of water to cool, with a hiss of steam. 'But the good ones like them are suffering now for the cruel and wicked ones.'

There were many things that Chantal found hard to believe as she lived week after week in the noisy, crowded house, and wandered with Philippe through teeming streets and stinking alleys where she had never been before and saw how the poor people of Paris had to live. In the great market where Lisette sold the few vegetables she could bring past the guards at the city gates, men and women and children crawled on the ground looking for cabbage stalks, bones, even egg shells.

The Revolution did not seem to have helped the poor people. There were beggars everywhere, cripples with bandages and crutches, showing off sores and injuries to get money. One night Chantal and Philippe were walking through the cemetery of the Holy Innocents to see if they believed in ghosts. In a yard behind a wall they saw some of the beggars taking off their wooden legs and bandages, washing off the red paint. This yard was called 'The Courtyard of Miracles' because the cripples were cured every night by removing their disguises.

But many people were really ill and many died of disease. Because of the dirt and crowding, there was a plague of smallpox. Lisette was afraid when the children went out, but she could not wash without water and they had to bring it to her in buckets hung in a sling from their shoulders. Chantal grew strong as well as dirty and ragged. If her mother ever did look out from some barred window high in a prison tower, would she even recognize her dainty daughter?

Once Chantal had seen the governess she

Chantal wandered with Philippe through teeming streets

used to hate because she rapped the back of her fingers when she got a sum wrong. The woman was wearing a tall hat with the red, white and blue cockade of the Revolution. She was on the arm of an officer with a white sash and boots and shoulder epaulettes like gold stair-brushes. Chantal ran past them through a puddle to splash the governess's long skirt. She shouted and aimed a blow, but she did not recognize the grubby urchin who ran laughing away.

Chapter Seven

'Don't go to the window, Chantal. Don't look.' Every day Lisette said this, but every day Chantal had to go down the passage to the window at the front of the house and crouch there to see the tumbrils go by. The tumbrils were two-wheeled hay carts in which the people who were going to be executed were taken past this house to the big Square where the guillotine stood.

As the tumbrils rumbled by, Chantal watched the brave, white faces. Nobles, politicians, common people, thieves, anyone who was suspected of being an enemy of the Revolution. When the line of carts reached the Square, a roar like jungle beasts went up from the crowd, and Chantal ran back to the kitchen where Lisette was ironing.

'I told you not to look, child.'

'I must. Because perhaps . . . Lisette, dear friend, tell me the truth. Don't you think that

Every day the tumbrils rumbled by

one day I might see my father and mother go by to the – to the—' She could not say the word.

'*No!*' Lisette stamped the iron down hard on the wet cloth, raising a cloud of steam.

'What will happen?' After her first storms

of weeping, there were no more tears left, only bravery.

'I don't know. They will deport them perhaps, send them away. Come on now, start folding these clothes. Sadness and worry won't buy us our bread.'

Lisette always tried to be calm, but one day she came back from the market in great agitation, panting and stammering, her pink cheeks scarlet, her gay brown eyes staring and afraid.

'Have you seen a ghost?'

Philippe was joking, but his mother said seriously, 'Worse than that. I saw *him*.'

'Who?'

'The traitor.'

'Marcel?'

'Ssh.' She put her finger to her lips and looked out to the yard where Henri the horse thief was leading in a grey Arab he had stolen. 'I hardly knew him. Smart Marcel in his bow tie and fancy waistcoat – now he's dressed like a citizen of the Revolution. Smock, baggy trousers, floppy red "Liberty bonnet" and all. I'd have laughed in his face, if I hadn't been afraid.'

'What did he say?'

'He said – you wouldn't believe it – he said, "I've always fancied you, Lisette. I'm going to come and visit you." '

Philippe and Chantal shrieked with laughter. 'Oh—' Philippe clapped his hand over his mouth. 'He's in love with you. That hideous Marcel! Did you curtsey, and say, "Charmed, my dear sir."?'

'Idiot! Don't be a cheeky boy. I said he could take his fancy talk to someone else.'

'She didn't fancy his fancy talk. Oh, fancy Marcel in his fancy red bonnet!' Chantal and Philippe laughed so hard that they rolled on the floor and kicked their heels and punched each other and giggled and worked themselves into that clowning state when just looking at each other made them collapse again and choke with laughter. There was so much sadness and worry in life that when there was something to laugh about, they overdid it.

'Stop it, you silly babies.' Lisette pulled Chantal to her feet and aimed a slap at Philippe which he ducked, still laughing about nothing at all. 'You don't understand.'

'We do understand, we do, we do.

Disgusting Marcel's in love with you!'

They pranced round her, red in the face with laughing.

'*He wants to come and look for Chantal.*'

They stopped like shot rabbits. Their faces dropped as if a hand had been passed down over them, wiping off the laughs. They stared at Lisette as she said urgently, 'We must get Chantal away at once, beyond the walls of Paris. She must come in the cart tomorrow when we go out to Saint Cloud for the chickens. I have my pass to get by the guards at the gate. Remember, you are my sister's daughter. I'll be taking you back to your mother.'

'My mother!' Chantal stopped staring and came to stand in front of Lisette with her jaw set and her eyes on fire. 'I'm not going to leave Paris. I'm not going to leave my mother and father.'

'What good is it to them if you are arrested too?' Lisette asked.

'I don't know. I don't know.' The fire went out of Chantal's eyes. She drooped her head. Only Philippe heard her whisper as she turned away, 'What good is life to me without them?'

Lisette, glad to be busy with plans, told Philippe to put new shoes on the horse before the journey out to the village of Saint Cloud.

'I'm out of nails.'

'Then go and get some, stupid boy.'

'I've got no money.'

'Who has? Get them the way you always do. Go and work the bellows for the blacksmith at the barracks.' She winked. Stealing from the soldiers was not called stealing. Weren't they the People's Army? 'On the way back, see if you can find bread. You can shoe the horse first thing tomorrow. Don't forget to mend the loose wagon wheel. And you, Chantal, go and bring two pails of water quickly to the washhouse and light the fire under the copper. I've got a lot of shirts to wash for the Captain before we go. Move, you lazy children! Out of here, I've got to sweep. Hurry up!' Soon she had everyone bustling round, which was the way she liked it, everyone doing things, not standing about and talking.

Chapter Eight

In the night when they all lay down on the piles of sacks and old rags which were their beds in this one room which was their home, Chantal lay awake, staring at the broken plaster of the ceiling, lit with mysterious shadowy flickers by the smouldering fire in the stove.

She could not sleep. Tomorrow another new life would begin. She would leave her last hope. Would she ever come back to Paris again? If they did send her parents away, how would she ever find them? How would they find her? And what if they had been hearing her whistle her song outside their prison walls? Would they still wait and listen every day?

In the darkness she pursed her lips and softly whistled the old nursery tune:

Co-Co was a naughty boy,
Co-Co was a brat . . .

Philippe crawled across the floor

The bundle of sacks on the other side of the room sat up. It was Philippe, also wide awake.

'Why aren't you asleep?' he whispered.

'How could I be?'

He crawled across the floor past Lisette, who was on her back, snoring as peacefully as if there were nothing wrong with the world.

'Listen.' He sat on the floor by Chantal and took her hand. 'There's something I've got to tell you. Yesterday when you were fetching the water, my mother told me a secret. She made me promise not to tell you, but I must. You're my best friend, Chantal.'

'And you're mine.' She squeezed his hand.

'Friends don't have secrets. I must tell you the truth.' He glanced over his shoulder at his sleeping mother. 'She told me that in the market she had asked Marcel, pretending, you know, not to be too much interested, "What will they do with your Count and Countess of Previn?" And Marcel laughed, that devilish laugh he has, like a hyena. "Don't call them mine," he said. "You can have them. Anyone can have them. And I'll tell you one thing," he said to my mother. "You'll never wash their linen again." '

'You mean they're going to be sent away?' Chantal whispered.

Philippe squeezed her hand. He didn't say anything.

'Tell me, Philippe. You said you'd tell me everything.'

'They're going to – to kill them.'

'Yes.' Chantal nodded. She felt quite cold and empty inside. 'I suppose I really knew that all the time.' After a frozen pause she asked, 'When?'

'Tomorrow. They're going to take them to the guillotine.'

They sat in silence and dread, holding hands in the dark, hearing the many night sounds of the crowded house. A baby crying, a man yelling at his wife. And the noises of the never-quiet street. Dogs barking, voices, shouts. Far off, a musket shot and a scream.

At last Philippe whispered, 'I'm sorry. I had to tell you what Marcel said. And then he said to my mother, "Are you quite *sure* you haven't seen that girl of theirs?" That's why you must escape tomorrow.'

'I won't go.'

'If you don't, they'll kill you too.'

'But they'll kill my parents if I do!' Suddenly the fear and pain that had clouded Chantal's brain had lifted away and everything became clear, like the rain-washed sunshine after a storm. 'Listen, Philippe. Listen.' She leaned forward and began to whisper fast. 'I've got an idea.'

Chapter Nine

The next morning, before the hour when the tumbrils usually went rumbling past the house on their way to the guillotine, Lisette made an excuse to go out.

'I hate to be here when the tumbrils pass by,' she said. 'Is there no stop to this terrible killing? When the Revolution started I thought it was the beginning of a better France for all of us. Liberty, equality, brotherhood! That's what they promised us. But now we've got this horror, this senseless cruelty . . .'

Chantal and Philippe knew why she was specially upset. But she did not know that they also knew who would be riding in the tumbrils this morning.

'You come with me, Chantal,' she said. 'We'll go and visit my poor old Aunt Sophie.'

'No, thank you.' Chantal put on a goody-goody face. 'I'd rather stay here and finish those sheets for you. You work so hard. I *want* to help. Please let me do your work.'

'Are you ill?' Lisette looked sharply at her, for usually Chantal did not like work any better than any other eleven-year-old girl. 'Well then, all right. Thank you. But stay out at the back of the house. I don't want you coming in to stare out of the front window. Remember now.'

Of course, Chantal knew why she said that. She looked at Philippe and he said, 'I'll stay with her to see she does the washing properly. I'll help her to hang out the sheets.'

'You won't!' His mother aimed one of her slaps at him that never hurt or even touched him because she did not really mean them to. 'You'll get out to the stable and shoe that horse. I told you to do it as soon as you got up. Why didn't you?'

'I'm sorry, Mother. Yes, Mother. Right away, Mother.' Philippe winked at Chantal as Lisette went out, scattering orders and warnings behind her like chicken-feed. So far everything was going according to plan. To their dangerous plan

When Lisette had gone off down the street, Chantal made up a big fire to heat the water in the copper and put in a load of sheets. She stirred them round with the heavy wooden paddle. When they were soaking wet, Philippe bundled two of them in his arms and climbed up the wooden staircase at the side of the house to hang them over the washing line that went across the end of the alley to the house on the other side.

Chantal put an old shawl round her head, which hid her red-gold hair and most of her face, and waited among the broken bottles and rubbish that people had thrown down under the rickety outside staircase where the alley led into the street.

From far away in the distance, she began to hear the hooves of heavy horses, and the rumble and clatter of the tumbril wheels coming towards her through the cobbled streets from the prison on the island.

Philippe was balanced high above her on a platform of the tumbledown stairs. She looked up and whistled like a goldfinch. He looked down and gave her a salute which meant, 'I'm ready. Courage.'

The sound of the horses and wagons came nearer, and with them the roaring and jeers of the crowds in the streets, although many of those who were going to their death were their own kind of people. Just ordinary people who had done nothing wrong. Perhaps they had once been friendly with an aristocrat. Perhaps they had dropped a careless criticism in a café about one of the new leaders. Perhaps they had helped a prisoner to escape. Perhaps they were too honest and gentle-hearted to suit the violent Revolutionaries. The roar of the crowd did not sound like human voices. The brutality of the Revolution was turning people into savage beasts.

There were seven wagons in line. Each one carried about ten men, women and even children standing up in them. Some wept, some clung to each other, some stared straight ahead so as not to give the savage crowd the pleasure of seeing that they were afraid.

One young woman had a baby in her arms. With her long, dark hair and her sweet face, pale and starved from prison, she looked like a statue of the Madonna with the baby, Jesus Christ.

Five, six, seven. Hiding under the stairs, Chantal searched desperately for the beloved

In the wagon were Chantal's mother and father

faces. They were not there. Marcel had been wrong. The plan was no good. Philippe looked down anxiously and she shook her head.

She was going to creep sadly away, but then the noise of the crowd grew louder again, and round the corner came one more tumbril, drawn by a plodding grey farm-horse. In the front of the wagon, standing proud and erect, holding onto the wooden slats meant to keep in a load of hay, were Chantal's mother and father.

Her father looked older. His thick brown hair was splashed with grey as if a paintbrush had been streaked through it. He was very thin and bony, his face pale as ashes, with a dismal beard round the firm chin that Chantal admired because her own chin was like it. His silk breeches and waistcoat and his ruffled shirt hung in filthy rags from his poor wasted body.

Her mother was as pale as a ghost, her lovely golden-red hair loose and tangled, her lilac dress stained and torn and covered with an old sack round her fragile shoulders.

'Mama!' Chantal cried out, as if her cry was her hands reaching forward. Luckily her voice was drowned in the shouts of the crowd, but her mother turned her face.

Then Chantal whistled a few notes of her special tune.

Co-Co was a naughty boy . . .

Her father, too, turned his head in wonder.

At that instant Philippe let go of the end of the washing line. The big, wet sheets dropped

The wet sheets dropped over the horse's head

over the horse's head. The horse kicked out at the wagon and struggled, slipping on the cobblestones.

The two guards marching at the back to keep away the crowd that pressed behind the tumbril ran up to the horse's head, but it fell, still smothered in sheets. The tumbril overturned and the people in it scrambled out and disappeared among the crowd.

Chapter Ten

The guards hunted everywhere. They broke into every house, pushed their way among the excited people, knocking heads with rifle butts if they got in the way, kicked over the rag and bone stall and the tables outside the tavern.

They searched every house from cellar to attic. When their boots came stamping down the alley and into the yard where Lisette's washhouse was, a small woman in a long black skirt with a scarf round her head was bending over the hot soapy water in the copper, stirring the paddle, her hair wet and straggling over her steamy face.

Chantal was staggering across the yard, half hidden by a pile of firewood.

'Who's that?' A guard grabbed her arm, and cursed as she dropped a chunk of wood on his foot.

'My aunt Lisette, of course. The washerwoman. Who else?'

In the forge at the side of the stable, the guards saw a bearded man wearing a leather apron over an old peasant's smock. On his head was the loose red 'liberty bonnet' of the citizens of the Revolution. Round his forehead almost over his eyes, was tied the piece of rag which a blacksmith wears to keep the sweat out of his eyes. He had the hind foot of the old brown horse between his knees as he bent over it and pounded with the big hammer.

'This horse kicks,' the blacksmith muttered

Philippe was at the handle of the bellows, pumping the furnace high so that the horseshoe in the fire throbbed and glowed. As one of the guards came near, he gave an extra push to the bellows and sent up a roar of hot air and a shower of fiery sparks.

'Look out!' the blacksmith muttered through a mouthful of nails. 'This brute of a horse kicks, you know.'

The guard stepped back and the other one pulled him away. 'Come on, let's not waste our time on these fools. If we don't find those cursed aristocrats, it'll be our necks next.'

They ran off down the alley as Lisette came into the yard from the street.

'Who's that at my copper?' she cried at once. She did not own much, but what she did, no one was going to make free with.

Chantal pulled her into the washhouse and shut the door. 'It's my mother.' And peering in wonder, Lisette saw.

With a gasp, she bent her knees to curtsey, but Chantal's mother took her hand and said, 'All that is in the past, my dear,' and they embraced, the Countess and the washerwoman who had saved her daughter.

Quickly Chantal told them both the rest of the plan for escape. 'Philippe is putting the horse into the cart. Now listen, Aunt Lisette. This is what we're going to do.'

Lisette listened, her eyes round with astonishment, and then she put a hand over her heart and said, 'No. It's too dangerous. I can't.'

Chantal stuck out her chin like her father. 'You must.'

'I can't.'

'Then they'll find my mother and father. And *then*' – she gripped Lisette by the arms and stood on tiptoe to put her face close to hers – 'we'll all be arrested too.'

The Count and Countess lay in the back of the cart, covered from head to foot with old potato sacks. Lisette, Chantal and Philippe climbed onto the seat in front. He flapped the reins on the horse's back and they were out of the yard and turning away down the alley, when Lisette, looking back, as she always did, to make sure her precious property had not caught fire the minute she left it, saw Marcel run out of the house door and into the yard.

She put her arm round Chantal's back to

hide her. 'Go to him, Philippe. Keep him there. Keep him away from the cart.'

The boy jumped down and strolled back into the yard, pretending to be casual.

'Where's your mother?' shouted Marcel in his rude way. 'I want some eggs. Get them for me.'

'How do I know she'd want to sell them to you?' Philippe asked. 'She only sells eggs to her friends.'

'Impudent dog! Shut your cheeky mouth. Where's your mother?'

'In the washhouse.'

'Ask her to come here.'

'Go and find her yourself.'

Furious, Marcel went into the washhouse. Philippe gave him a mighty push in the back, followed by a kick for luck, slammed the door and fastened an iron bar across it.

He ran back to the cart, jumped up and picked up the reins, and they drove off to the sounds of Marcel's furious shouts and kicks and pounding on the door.

Chapter Eleven

Philippe hurried the old horse as fast as he would go through the back streets. They came to the gate in the city wall and stopped. One of the soldiers who had been leaning against the gate came forward, and Lisette showed him the paper which was her pass to go to and from Saint Cloud.

'What have you got in the back there?' The soldier's voice was thick and foolish. In one hand he held his gun, with the long bright bayonet fixed, in the other, a bottle of wine.

'They are very ill. Victims of the pox. Poor souls.' Lisette wagged her head. 'They won't last much longer. We've been asked to take them out of the city to where they can't infect so many people. They were our neighbours, so alas, we may be infected too.'

She and Philippe and Chantal were all wearing large handkerchiefs over their noses and mouths, as people had to do when they had been in contact with someone who had the disease.

The soldier stepped back. Everyone in Paris was terrified of catching the pox. 'Get away from here then, you and the boy. And who's that?' He pointed at Chantal. With the shawl round her head and the handkerchief round the bottom part of her face, he could only see her eyes.

'My niece from Saint Cloud. Don't you remember when I brought her into the city with me some months ago? You must have been drunk.'

'I'm drunk now, if you want to know.' The guard took a gurgling swill out of the wine bottle. 'We're all drunk. Drunk with the wine of power and liberty. Drunk on the blood that the guillotine has poured out to us from our enemies. Drive on, citizen Lisette!'

He pulled open the gate. A few more yards and they would be through. Chantal's heart was singing, but as the horse started forward, the other soldier, younger, sharper, not drunk, caught at the bridle.

'Just a moment, Corporal. Our orders are to check everything. I'd better look in the

The horse jerked them forward into freedom

back of the cart, even if you're too full of wine to bother.'

'And give us all the pox?' the Corporal shouted. 'Fool! Idiot! Traitor to France!' With the butt of his gun, he knocked the soldier's hand away from the bridle. 'Get going, boy!' he shouted to Philippe. 'Get your load of pox out of our way.' He pulled out a red and white spotted kerchief and put it over his face. 'And remember' – his voice came through, thick and muffled – 'after this, you can't come back!'

'We know,' Chantal whispered, and she was glad that she wore the handkerchief over her mouth, so that he could not see her smile of joy and hope as Philippe slapped the reins and the horse jerked them forward into freedom.